"Chippy Chipmunk,"
an eastern chipmunk
(actual size)

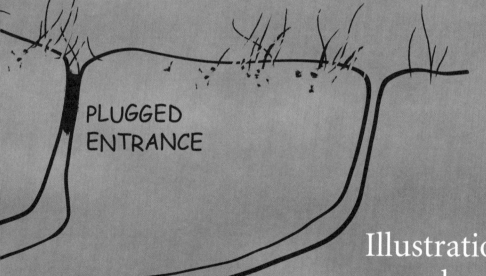

PLUGGED
ENTRANCE

Illustration of a
complex chipmunk burrow

CHIPPY CHIPMUNK

Friends in the Garden

Written and photographed by Kathy M. Miller

♡ Kathy M. Miller

To my friends, you are flowers in the garden of my life.

To those experiencing loss, may nature be a source of comfort to you.

To Denise Whalen, a special thanks for suggesting I write this book to help children.

Thanks to the following professionals who work with children and who either made a contribution to or offered suggestions for this book: Denise Whalen, Melissa Carr, Mike Evans, Karen Sugrue, Laura Yazemboski, Kathy Benson, Holly Carson, and Mary Crawford.

Thanks to Lynne Curry and Arian Hungaski for their editorial assistance.

Published by:

Celtic Sunrise

PO Box 174, New Ringgold, PA 17960

570 943 2102

www.celticsunrise.com

First Edition   10 9 8 7 6 5 4 3 2 1

For children 4 & older and the young at heart.
If chewed, the cover, jacket, or laminated coating could fragment and become a potential choking hazard.

Publisher's Cataloging-in-Publication Data

Miller, Kathy M.
    Chippy Chipmunk : friends in the garden / written and photographed by Kathy M. Miller.
        pages cm. – (Chippy Chipmunk series)
    ISBN: 978-0-9840893-2-1 (hardcover)
    1. Chipmunks—Juvenile fiction. 2. Loss (Psychology)—Fiction. 3. Hope—Fiction.   I. Title.
PZ7.M62225 Ch 2015
[Fic]—dc23
                            2014910871

www.chippychipmunk.com

Book design by Rob Mull Design   www.robmull.com

Prepress production in Ohio

Printed in China

This book is printed in compliance with the Consumer Products Safety Improvement Act (CPSIA).
Printed August, 2014   Reference Number 50005140

ISBN-13 978-0-9840893-2-1
ISBN-10 0-9840893-2-2

When seasons changed from summer to fall,
some of Chippy Chipmunk's friends began their
long journey south to where the weather was warm.

It was a cool, clear morning when the hummingbird came to say goodbye. He took one last sip of nectar and set off on his epic 3,000-mile migration to Mexico.

"See you in the spring!" squealed Chippy as the tiny bird zipped away.

He may have had to say goodbye to some of his friends but he also made a new, funny one.

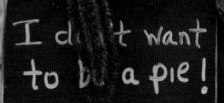

I don't want to be a pie!

One day, Chippy played "I Spy" with his friends. "I spy with my little eye," he called, "an elephant that can fly!"

"In the sky!"
    answered his buddy with the sharpest eye.

After a while, Chippy decided to
look for his best friend Pickle,
a meadow vole.

He looked in all the usual places but couldn't find him anywhere.

After a few hours of searching, he tucked himself in, closed his eyes, and curled up to take a short nap. Suddenly, he heard a loud "THUMP."

The rabbit had come to deliver some very sad news.

Pickle had died.

"Was it a cat?" asked Chippy.

"No," the rabbit replied.

Earlier that day, a crafty red fox had
snatched his prey,

then slowly,
sneakily crept away.

The rabbit cried

and Chippy cried too.

His friends didn't know what to say. So the squirrel gathered some seeds for him. The bluebird picked him a fresh, juicy berry.

The goldfinch chose the smoothest flower petal to give Chippy and then she offered him a turn on the swing.

But Chippy wasn't hungry.
He didn't want to play.

"Am I going to die too?" he worried.
"I'm going to watch out for that fox."

The house finch began to chirp softly.
"I'm sorry about Pickle. When I sing one of my favorite songs, it makes me feel a little better."

Then the porcupine had an idea. She always knew what to do. "Let's dedicate a special place in memory of Pickle. The carved wooden bear will be the perfect spot as that was Pickle's favorite nook."

They gathered at the bear where they shared funny stories and smiled at happy memories of their friend. Pickle had been a kind meadow vole and they vowed to be kind too.

Chippy made a wish
that his friend was
now soaring like an
eagle. Pickle had
always wanted to fly.

"Where did Pickle go?" asked one of the speckled baby bluebirds. "Up beyond the clouds, where everything is wonderful," replied her father.

Snow came early that year and since Chippy wasn't much in the mood to collect nuts, he decided to hibernate early. He crawled into his underground burrow for his long winter nap.

The cardinal thought of something nice they could do for their friend and couldn't wait to share his idea.

Everyone helped to take up a food collection for Chippy!

Eastern Bluebird

Black-capped Chickadee

Pileated Woodpecker

American Goldfinch

Eastern Gray Squirrel

Northern Mockingbird

Northern Cardinal

Meanwhile, Chippy, all snug in his nest and deep in sleep, began to dream. They were vivid, magical dreams.

A barred owl appeared first.
"*Every day gets better*," he said,
"but it takes time. Look for
things that remind you of Pickle."

The great gray owl appeared next. *"Those we love live forever in our hearts.* Think of this whenever you see a heart.

Do you see one now?"

Two imaginative snowy owls were the last to appear in his dreams.

"It helps us to think that beautiful things are sent to us from up beyond the clouds."

Months later when the birds announced the arrival of spring, Chippy emerged from his burrow. He began to play with those thoughtful friends who had gathered berries for him while he slept. Chippy still missed Pickle but he knew he would never forget him. He always kept an eye out for something to remind him of Pickle.

Then a fantastic sight
appeared in the sky!

A giant eagle floated by.

Every day gets better,
thought Chippy.

Those we love live forever in our hearts.
Find the hearts in these photos.

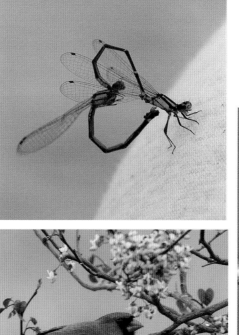

Now you draw whoever lives forever in your heart.
Do you have a favorite memory?

Note to Parents:

The loss of a loved one is hard at any age. A child's grief may look very different from that of an adult's, often presenting as an emotion that seems to be completely unrelated to the situation. Children may find expressing what they are experiencing difficult to do. They are frequently reluctant to share their feelings because they may not want to upset the adults around them who already seem sad. Here are some thoughts to keep in mind to help a child who has suffered a loss:

- Grieving children may appear angry and demonstrate aggressive behavior. This is not uncommon, and it is a way for children not to have to express the underlying feelings that are scarier.

- Children are often afraid that they will upset others by discussing the loved one. It is important to give children permission to talk about the individual by letting them know that all feelings are okay. Reassure the children it's all right to speak about their emotions and share stories about their memories. Let them express their feelings through art or play.

- Children also worry that they will forget the person that passed. A "memory box" containing objects that are reminders of the loved one who is no longer with them is helpful, as well as a "joy journal," a notebook containing happy or funny memories of the cherished individual.

- Don't be afraid to ask for help in dealing with the loss.
  Several good online resources that may be beneficial include the following:
  childrengrieve.org - National Alliance for Grieving Children
  dougy.org - The Dougy Center: The National Center for Grieving Children & Families

- Your pediatrician is also a resource to help provide you with assistance and local referral sources for children's therapists if necessary.

  Remember, although loss affects everyone, talking about it is crucial. While encouraging children to express their feelings is essential, it's also important to reinforce the message that "Every day gets better!"

  Denise L. Whalen, M.A., Licensed Professional Counselor, National Certified Counselor

Location of hearts:

  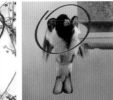   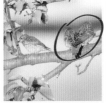  

Eastern Wild Turkeys   Pileated Woodpecker   Rose-breasted Grosbeak   Eastern Bluebirds   Yellow-rumped Warbler   Eastern Bluebirds   Eastern Cottontail   American Goldfinches   Northern Flicker

Note to Educators:

Storybooks about grief may be helpful for a student who experienced a loss. They may also be used as a *read aloud* to a classroom that has suffered from the death of a student within their class or school. Offering some type of commemorative activity following the reading would give students an opportunity to express their own feelings through writing or artwork.

Here are some guidelines to help you be more aware and sensitive to students' grief:

- Listen. Let the students tell you their feelings and describe what their grief is like for them. Do not assume you know how they feel as emotions will vary and change with time.

- Don't worry about saying the right thing or having all the answers. Just "being there" for them will help. An empathetic response like "I'm sorry" is best.

- Saying "Every day gets better!" has been helpful in my work with grieving children because it's easy for them to remember.

- Be patient. Know that your students may be withdrawn or have difficulty in your classroom as they adjust to their loss.

- Follow your daily routines as usual in your classroom as much as possible. The quicker they get back to their normal routine, the easier their adjustment.

- Every student deals with grief in a different way. There is no right or wrong method for coping with grief.

- Create an environment full of support and acceptance in your classroom.

- Encourage your students to share their memories about the loss they experienced.

- When students grieve, it is not a "one-time thing." It is a process that takes time for students to develop ways that help them handle their emotions.

Grief is a difficult journey for any student to experience. While each journey is unique for every individual, you can be a valuable guide to provide support in the healing process!

Melissa Carr, M.Ed., Elementary School Counselor

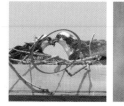
Ospreys

Eastern Bluebird

Tufted Titmouse

Eastern Chipmunks

Eastern Bluebird

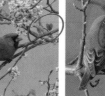
Damselflies

Northern Cardinal

Eastern Bluebirds

Downy Woodpecker

There are more than 20 hummingbird species in North America and over 300 worldwide. The ruby-throated hummingbird commonly migrates to southern Mexico. Those that cross the Gulf of Mexico must endure a grueling, nonstop 500-mile flight that can take 24 hours.!

This rainbow is over water. Have fun with your family making your own rainbow. Science books or science websites that are geared for children provide instructions about how to create one using several different methods.

Voles are small rodents that commonly use burrows. They measure 3-9 inches in length depending on the species.

In fall, Osage oranges turn bright yellow-green. This bumpy fruit is in the mulberry family. They are considered inedible due to their peculiar taste.

Fun facts about chipmunks are included in the books: *Chippy Chipmunk Parties in the Garden* and *Chippy Chipmunk: Babies in the Garden*

This corn was fresh from a local farm and was not harmful to wildlife. Seasonal decorations can be harmful if they are moldy or have been treated with chemical preservatives.

To see chipmunks, visit Hawk Mountain Sanctuary between April and November. www.hawkmountain.org
The wooden bear was created by Chainsaw Carving Artist, Todd Gladfelter, New Ringgold, PA. www.redmountainarts.net
The resting fox was in the care of the Elmwood Park Zoo, Norristown, PA. www.elmwoodparkzoo.org
The sneaking fox, porcupine, and snowy owls were in the care of the Ecomuseum Zoo, Ste-Anne-de-Bellevue, QC. www.zooecomuseum.ca
The great horned owl on the facing page was in the care of the Red Creek Wildlife Center, Schuylkill Haven, PA. www.redcreekwildlifecenter.com
The publisher will plant trees to offset those used to produce this book.